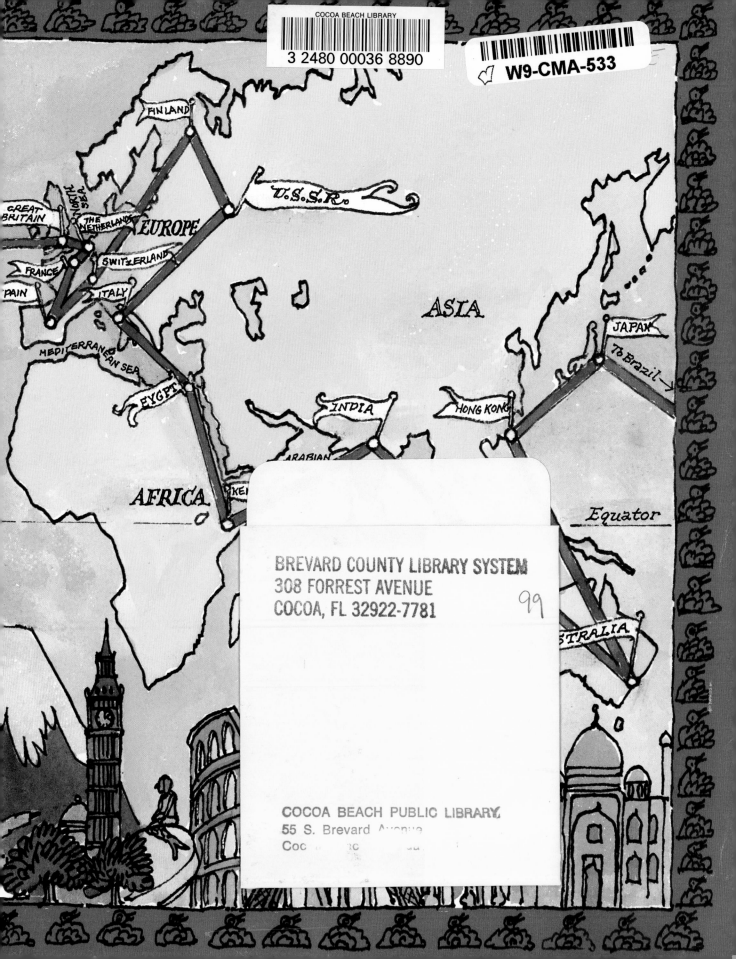

It all started one evening at Clara's....

HENRY'S WORLD TOUR

Story and Pictures by Robert Quackenbush

A Doubleday Book for Young Readers

A Doubleday Book for Young Readers
Published by
Delacorte Press
Bantam Doubleday Dell Publishing Group, Inc.
666 Fifth Avenue
New York, New York 10103
Doubleday and the portrayal of an anchor with a dolphin
are trademarks of Bantam Doubleday Dell Publishing Group, Inc.

Library of Congress Cataloging in Publication Data
Quackenbush, Robert M.
Henry's world tour / story and pictures by Robert Quackenbush.
p.   cm.
Summary: Henry the Duck embarks on a round-the-world tour, visiting
relatives everywhere to find out why he has one speckled feather in his tail.
ISBN: 0-385-42010-2
[1. Ducks—Fiction. 2. Voyages around the world—Fiction.]
I. Title.
PZ7.Q16Hg 1992
[E]—dc20   91-31257
                                                                CIP
                                                                AC

Manufactured in the United States of America
September 1992
10   9   8   7   6   5   4   3   2   1
LBM

For Henry fans
everywhere

One morning Henry the Duck
woke up and saw a
speckled feather growing
from his tail.
He wondered how he got it.
He called his friend, Clara.
He had been over at her house
for dinner the night before.
They saw each other often and
told each other everything.

"You should check your
roots, Henry," said Clara.
"Maybe one of your ancestors
had speckled feathers."
Henry knew that his ancestors
came from all over the world.
He had cousins living in
many different countries.
He decided to go visit some
of them to find out where
he got his speckled feather.

Henry traveled across the
great Atlantic Ocean to visit
his British cousins in London.
They took him to see the
changing of the guard at
Buckingham Palace.
Henry tried so hard to peer
through the fence that his
head got stuck between two bars.
He had to be wrestled free.
Poor Henry left England with
a pinched head, a sore neck,
and no leads about his
speckled feather.

Next, Henry crossed the
North Sea to the Netherlands.
While sightseeing with his
Dutch cousins, he got caught
in a whirling windmill.
Not only that, the tulips
everywhere gave him hay fever:

QUAAACK-CHOOO!

He left his cousins with a
runny beak and no facts about
where his speckled feather
came from.

Henry traveled on to France
to visit cousins in Paris.
They went to dine at Maxim's.
But Henry tripped and fell
smack into the desserts.
Apricot tarts and chocolate
mousse went flying all over.
Henry ended up with mousse
in his face and not a hint
about his speckled feather.

Henry went south to sunny
Spain to see cousins
who worked at a bull ring.
Poor Henry went through
the wrong gate.
He got chased by a bull
and poked by a *picadilla*!
Picked and poked was
all Henry got.
His cousins had no tips
to give him about his
speckled feather.

High on the mighty Alps
of Switzerland, Henry got
involved with a bunch
of yodeling relatives:

 QUACK-A-LAY-DE-HOO ♫

They nearly burst
Henry's eardrums.
On top of that, they'd never
heard of ancestors with
speckled feathers.

Onward Henry traveled to
the far north of Finland.
He visited cousins who
were into health and fitness.
"Try our sauna!" they said.
They roasted him in a
hot house and then threw
him in an ice pond.
They knew all about
keeping in shape, but
they knew nothing about
Henry's speckled feather.

Henry's next stop was
the U.S.S.R. to visit his
Russian cousins in Moscow.
They also could shed no light
on his speckled feather.
But they loved him so, they
tossed him in the air and
spun him around until his
eyes crossed.

Worn out, Henry headed
for Italy hoping for
some peace and quiet.
No such luck.
His Italian cousins were
so glad to see him that
they partied loudly and
stuffed him full of pasta.
But they had no news to
give him about his
speckled feather.

Crossing the Mediterranean
Sea, Henry landed in Egypt.
While he was taking
pictures of the pyramids,
a camel came and sat on him.
Henry left his cousins,
squished and squashed and
with no family history about
his speckled feather.

Down to the Equator in
East Africa went Henry.
His cousins in Kenya
took him on a photo safari.
Horrors!
Henry was nearly gobbled
up by a lion!
Weak and trembling, Henry
left Africa, too, with nothing
to tell Clara about his
speckled feather.

Henry crossed the
Arabian Sea to India.
His cousins gave him
a turban to wrap around
his head, but Henry got
himself wrapped up instead.
Even worse, his cousins
had no records of ancestors
with speckled feathers.

Henry went below the
Equator to Australia.
In the vast outback
country, he was chased
by a mob of kangaroos.
One of the mothers thought
Henry was kidnapping her baby.
But the baby was kidnapping him!
Fortunately, Henry's cousins
came to his rescue.
But they had no idea where
he got his speckled feather.

Henry headed north to
visit cousins in Hong Kong.
After an eighteen-dish
meal, he went for a ride
in a rickshaw.
Big mistake!
Henry was bounced about so
in heavy traffic that he
got a terrible tummy ache.
Pea-green and dizzy, he
left his cousins without
even a clue about his
speckled feather.

Arriving in Japan, Henry
was given a kimono and
wooden shoes—called *geta*.
During a tea ceremony,
he forgot to leave his
shoes outside the door.
He tripped on his kimono
and crashed into a
valuable tea set.
Limping and hobbling,
Henry left his cousins
with a twisted ankle
and no information about
his speckled feather.

Henry traveled across
the mighty Pacific Ocean
to South America, to
visit cousins in Brazil.
Goodness, such excitement!
They kept him dancing the
samba and the lambada
until he threw his
hip out of joint.
But they couldn't tell
him anything about his
speckled feather.

At last Henry headed for home.
Sore and worn out as he was,
he went to Clara's house and told
her everything that had happened.
"But Henry," said Clara. "I
found out about your speckled
feather after you left.
Remember when you were having
dinner at my house the night
before you noticed the feather?
Well...

...I found out that you sat on
a chair I freshly painted."

The End

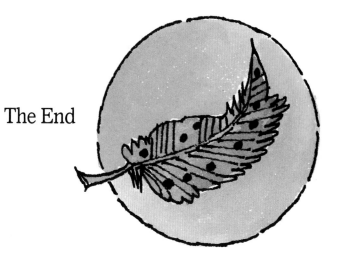